JACK PRELUTSKY

The Dragons Are Singing Tonight

PICTURES BY

PETER SÍS

A MULBERRY PAPERBACK BOOK · NEW YORK

The full-color art was reproduced from oil and
gouache paintings on a gesso background.
The text type is Carnese Medium.

The Library of Congress has cataloged the Greenwillow Books
edition of *The Dragons Are Singing Tonight* as follows:

Prelutsky, Jack.
The dragons are singing tonight /
by Jack Prelutsky ; pictures by Peter Sís.
p. cm.
Summary: A collection of poems about dragons,
including "I'm an Amiable Dragon,"
"If You Don't Believe in Dragons,"
and "A Dragon Is in My Computer."
ISBN 0-688-09645-X (trade)
ISBN 0-688-12511-5 (lib. bdg.)
1. Dragons—Juvenile Poetry.
2. Children's poetry, American.
[1. Dragons—Poetry. 2. American poetry.]
I. Sís, Peter, ill.
II.Title.
PS3566.R36D7 1993
811'.54—dc20
92-29013 CIP AC

3 5 7 9 10 8 6 4
First Mulberry Edition, 1998
ISBN 0-688-16162-6

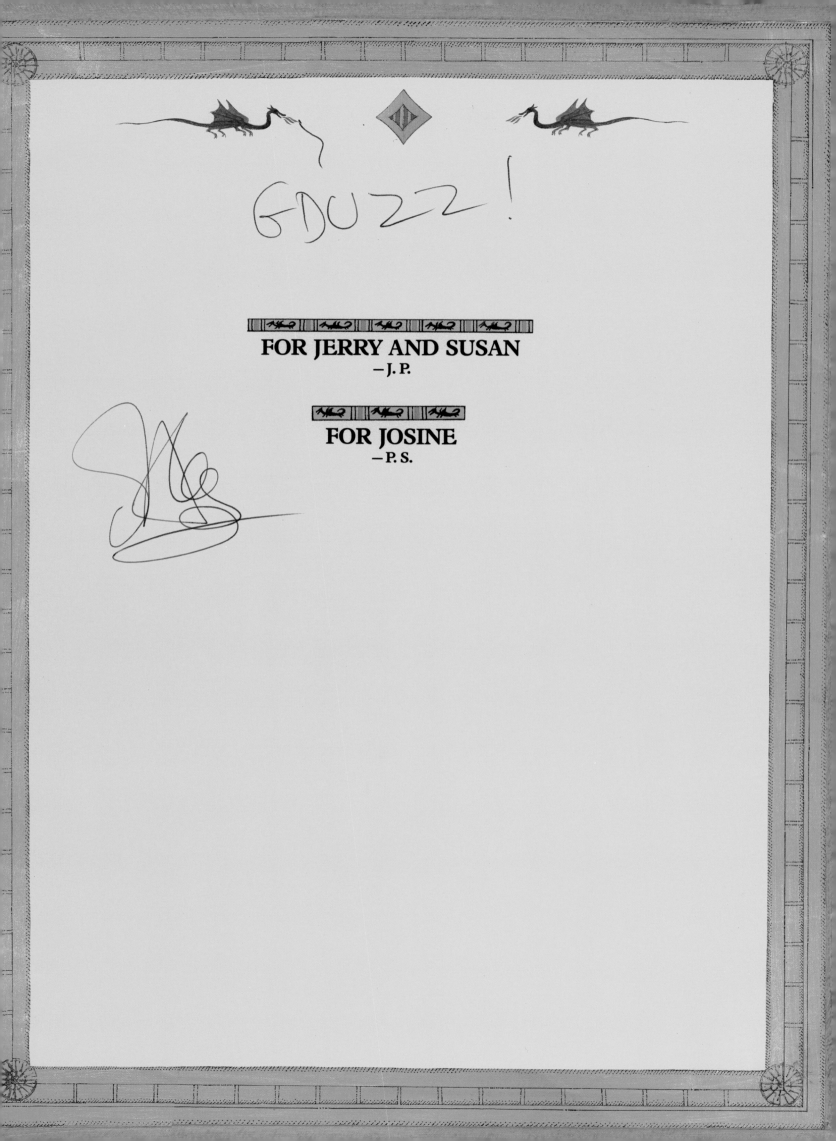

GDUZZ!

FOR JERRY AND SUSAN
—J. P.

FOR JOSINE
—P. S.

CONTENTS

I'M AN AMIABLE DRAGON

I'm an amiable dragon,
And I have no wish to scare,
Do not tremble at my presence,
Do ignore my lethal stare,
Do not fret about the fire
I unleash into the air,
You are free to pass unchallenged —
But only if you dare!

7

I AM WAITING WAITING WAITING

I am waiting waiting waiting for my dragon egg to hatch,
I've been waiting waiting waiting for a year,
Ever since I found it hidden in my mother's garden patch —
Now I think my baby dragon's almost here.

I have never had a dragon of my very own before,
And I wonder, will my dragon breathe a flame?
Will it greet me every morning with a friendly little roar?
Will it answer when I summon it by name?

I am counting off the seconds till my dragon first appears,
Poking through the shell to freedom with a horn,
I can't wait to see its winglets, tiny muzzle, tail and ears,
When my brand new baby dragon's finally born.

IF YOU DON'T BELIEVE IN DRAGONS

If you don't believe in dragons,
It is curiously true
That the dragons you disparage
Choose to not believe in you.

I WISH I HAD A DRAGON

I wish I had a dragon
With diamond-studded scales,
With claws like silver sabers,
And fangs like silver nails,
A dragon fierce and faithful,
Always ready by my side,
A dragon to defend me
Or to take me for a ride.

I wish I had a dragon
With eyes of shining gold,
Who breathed a plume of fire
Whenever it was told,
A dragon so ferocious
It might frighten Frankenstein,
But not a lazy dragon
Who sleeps all day...like mine!

I MADE A MECHANICAL DRAGON

I made a mechanical dragon
Of bottle tops, hinges, and strings,
Of thrown-away clocks and unmendable socks,
Of hangers and worn innersprings.
I built it of cardboard and plastic,
Of doorknobs and cables and corks,
Of spools and balloons and unusable spoons,
And rusty old shovels and forks.

It's quite an unusual dragon
It rolls on irregular wheels,
It clatters and creaks and it rattles and squeaks,
And when it tips over, it squeals.
I've tried to control its maneuvers,
It fails to obey my commands,
It bumps into walls till it totters and falls—
I made it myself with my hands!

NASTY LITTLE DRAGONSONG

I'm a nasty, nasty dragon,
I've been nasty since my birth,
When it comes to nasty dragons,
I'm the nastiest on earth.
I've a nasty, nasty temper,
And my breath is nasty too,
I was nasty to my parents,
I'll be nastier to you.

It's my nature to be nasty,
Nasty, nasty night and day,
I will act completely nasty
If you're in my nasty way.
Yet I largely pass unnoticed
As I nastily go by,
I'm a nasty, nasty dragon
Just a nasty half inch high.

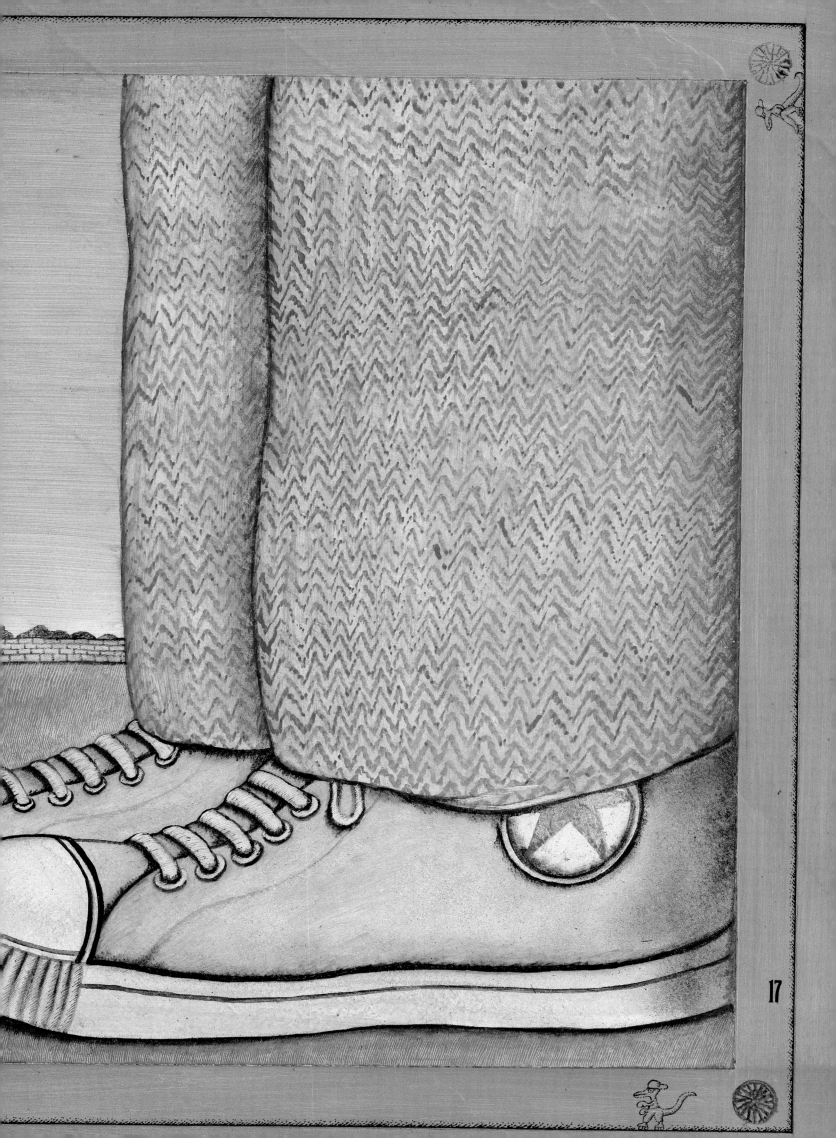

MY DRAGON WASN'T FEELING GOOD

My dragon wasn't feeling good,
He had a nasty chill
And couldn't keep from shivering,
I saw that he was ill.
His eyes were red and watery,
His nose was running too,
His flame was but a fizzle,
And his cheeks were pallid blue.

I took him to a doctor
Just as quickly as I could,
A specialist in dragons,
And she's in our neighborhood.
She took his pulse and temperature,
Then fed him turpentine
And phosphorus and gasoline—
My dragon's doing fine.

I AM MY MASTER'S DRAGON

I am my master's dragon,
And my master treats me well,
He calls me when he wants me,
And I answer to his bell.
He feeds me puffs of pastry
To reward me for my deeds,
And according to my master,
I have all a dragon needs.

My master fails to notice,
Though I know that he is smart,
The incalculable sadness
Deep within my dragon heart.
But I am not complaining,
I've no sorry tale to tell,
I am my master's dragon,
And my master treats me well.

21

THE DRAGONS ARE SINGING TONIGHT

Tonight is the night all the dragons
Awake in their lairs underground,
To sing in cacophonous chorus
And fill the whole world with their sound.
They sing of the days of their glory,
They sing of their exploits of old,
Of maidens and knights, and of fiery fights,
And guarding vast caches of gold.

Some of their voices are treble,
And some of their voices are deep,
But all of their voices are thunderous,
And no one can get any sleep.
I lie in my bed and I listen,
Enchanted and filled with delight,
To songs I can hear only one night a year—
The dragons are singing tonight.

23

DRAGONBRAG

Once upon a happenstance
I met a knight in armor.
I fixed my flame upon his lance —
It was a four-alarmer!

25

A DRAGON'S LAMENT

I'm tired of being a dragon,
Ferocious and brimming with flame
The cause of unspeakable terror
When anyone mentions my name.
I'm bored with my bad reputation
For being a miserable brute,
And being routinely expected
To brazenly pillage and loot.

I wish that I weren't repulsive,
Despicable, ruthless, and fierce,
With talons designed to dismember
And fangs finely fashioned to pierce.
I've lost my desire for doing
The deeds any dragon should do,
But since I can't alter my nature,
I guess I'll just terrify you.

I HAVE A DOZEN DRAGONS

I have a dozen dragons,
I bought them at the mall,
I keep them in my closet,
It's fortunate they're small.
Their horns are red and silver,
Their scales are green and gold,
All of them are beautiful,
And all of them are bold.

They eat vanilla ice cream,
And pickles mixed with ink,
Then run around the kitchen
And jump into the sink.
They splash about the basin
And flap their silver wings,
While breathing tiny fires
That never burn a thing.

When we go out on weekends
And stroll around the block,
The neighbors stare in wonder,
They seem to be in shock.
I may not have a puppy,
A kitten, or a bird,
But I'm the only one I know
Who has a dragon herd.

I AM BOOM!

I am Boom the thunder dragon,
Taller than the tallest trees,
I stir whirlwinds when I whisper,
Mighty cyclones when I sneeze,
Fishes shiver in the ocean
When I tread upon the shore,
I make earthquakes and volcanoes
When I roar roar **roar!**

I am Boom the thunder dragon,
All the earth is my domain,
When I flap my wings in fury,
I create a hurricane,
Lions vanish at my footsteps,
Eagles tremble at my glance,
And the mountains start to rumble
When I dance dance **dance!**

Giants fly into a panic
When I rear my massive head,
When I snort my searing fires,
Fearless ogres faint with dread,
If you ever see me coming,
You had better give me room,
I am Boom the thunder dragon,
I am BOOM! BOOM! **BOOM!**

A DRAGON IS IN MY COMPUTER

A dragon is in my computer,
It's there when I turn on the screen,
It stares at me, fierce and unfriendly,
Through eyes of malevolent green.
It hisses and spits little fires,
It flicks its preposterous tail,
I've tried every trick to erase it,
But all of my stratagems fail.

It's there when I'm doing my homework,
It's there when I'm playing a game,
My mouse does its best to erase it,
That dragon remains all the same.
It may disappear for a minute,
But always comes slithering back,
Appearing on top of my program,
Resuming its nasty attack.

I have no idea where it came from,
Or why it keeps picking on me,
Examining me like a morsel
It's thinking it might fricassee.
I wish I could douse it with water
And bop it a bit on the snout,
A dragon is in my computer —
I hope that it never gets out.

I HAVE A SECRET DRAGON

I have a secret dragon
Who is living in the tub,
It greets me when I take a bath,
And gives my back a scrub.
My parents cannot see it,
They don't suspect it's there,
They look in its direction,
And all they see is air.

My dragon's very gentle,
My dragon's very kind,
No matter how I pull its tail,
My dragon doesn't mind.
We splash around together
And play at silly things,
Then when I'm finished bathing,
It dries me with its wings.

MY DRAGON'S BEEN DISCONSOLATE

My dragon's been disconsolate
And cannot help but pout,
Since he defied a thunderstorm
That put his fire out.

ONCE THEY ALL BELIEVED IN DRAGONS

Once they all believed in dragons
When the world was fresh and young,
We were woven into legends,
Tales were told and songs were sung,
We were treated with obeisance,
We were honored, we were feared,
Then one day they stopped believing —
On that day, we disappeared.

Now they say our time is over,
Now they say we've lived our last,
Now we're treated with derision
Where we once ruled unsurpassed.
We must make them all remember,
In some way we must reveal
That our spirit lives forever —
We are dragons! We are real!

There can be very few children
under twelve in America
who have not encountered
JACK PRELUTSKY.
He is one of the most frequently
anthologized poets writing
today. He has written over thirty
books of verse, edited several
hugely popular anthologies,
and has appeared in more
schools and libraries than he
can count. Among his most
popular books are *Something
Big Has Been Here, The New
Kid on the Block,* and
Tyrannosaurus Was a Beast.
He and his wife live in
the Seattle area.

PETER SÍS
was born in Czechoslovakia
and lives in New York City.
He was educated in Prague and
London, and his films have
received honors throughout the
world. His drawings appear
regularly in the *New York Times
Book Review* and other
publications. He is the author-
artist of *Komodo!, An Ocean
World, Follow the Dream, Beach
Ball,* and other popular books.
Books he has illustrated include
The Whipping Boy by Sid
Fleischman and *Stories to Solve*
by George Shannon.